I0708823

COSCON
ENTERTAINMENT

Also by A.P. Fuchs

Blood of My World Trilogy

Discovery of Death
Memories of Death
Life of Death

Undead World Trilogy

Blood of the Dead
Possession of the Dead
Redemption of the Dead

The Axiom-man™ Saga
(listed in reading order)

Axiom-man
Episode No. 0: First Night Out
Doorway of Darkness
Episode No. 1: The Dead Land
City of Ruin
Episode No. 2: Underground Crusade
Outlaw
Of Magic and Men (comic book)

Mech Apocalypse

Mech Apocalypse

Other Fiction

A Stranger Dead
A Red Dark Night
April (writing as Peter Fox)
Magic Man (deluxe chapbook)
The Way of the Fog (The Ark of Light Vol. 1)

Devil's Playground (written with Keith Gouveia)
On Hell's Wings (written with Keith Gouveia)
Zombie Fight Night: Battles of the Dead
Magic Man Plus 15 Tales of Terror
Undeniable
The Dance of Mervo and Father Clown

Anthologies (as editor)

Dead Science
Elements of the Fantastic
Vicious Verses and Reanimated Rhymes: Zany
Zombie Poetry for the Undead Head
Metahumans vs the Undead
Bigfoot Terror Tales Vol. 1 (with Eric S. Brown)
Bigfoot Terror Tales Vol. 2 (with Eric S. Brown)
Metahumans vs Werewolves

Non-fiction

Book Marketing for the
Financially-challenged Author
Canadian Scribbler: Collected Letters of an
Underground Writer
Look, Up on the Screen! The Big Book of
Superhero Movie Reviews
Getting Down and Digital: How to Self-publish
Your Book
The Canister X Transmission: Year One

Poetry

The Hand I've Been Dealt
Haunted Melodies and Other Dark Poems
Still About A Girl

WWW.CANISTERX.COM

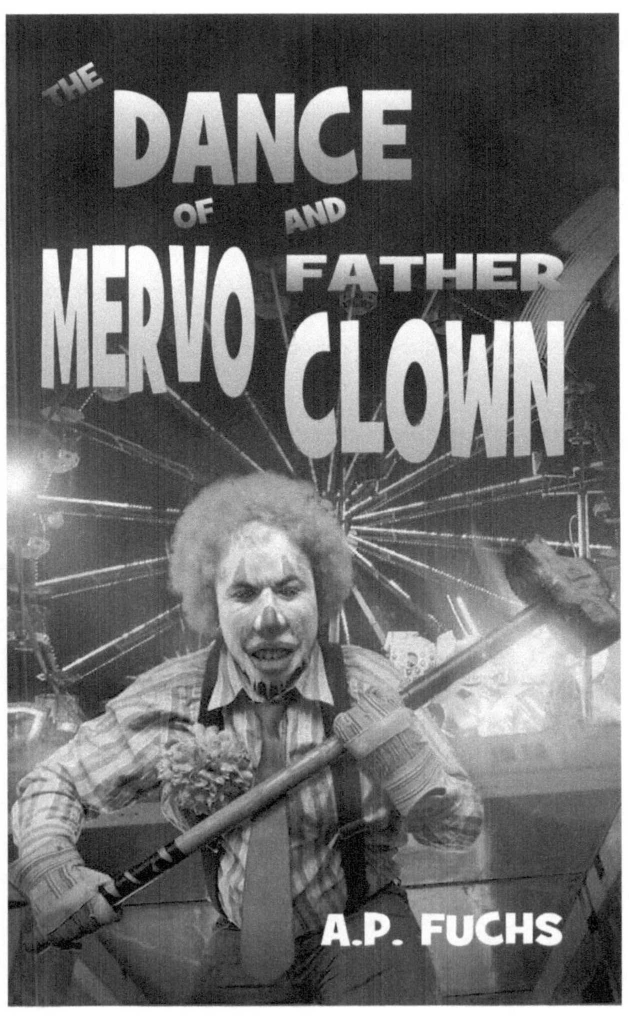

COSCOM ENTERTAINMENT
WINNIPEG

ISBN 978-1-927339-57-2

Published by COSCOM ENTERTAINMENT

Text set in Garamond; Printed and bound in the USA

COVER ART BY C.J. HUTCHINSON AND
JESUS MORALES/DARK RIDDLE

A.P. FUCHS WEBSITE: www.canisterx.com

This thriller under the big top is for Anthony Giangregorio, without whose invitation this story wouldn't have been written. Thanks for being a pal and inspiration.

The Dance of Mervo and Father Clown

1

"No way, I won't go in there!" Jackson screamed. Even at nine years old he knew better than to go into a haunted house.

"So, what, you're going to spend the rest of your life afraid?" his father asked. His old man's piercing blue eyes gazed into his. His dad had a way of looking tough, even when wearing a black Scooby Doo ball cap.

His dad had disappointment etched on his face, and while Jackson understood his old man wanted him to be strong, he had a hard time believing he could muster the strength to go inside such a scary place.

From the outside, the haunted house was enormous: big black and wide, against a backdrop of trees. The creepy visage of a goblin with yellow eyes loomed over him, the words HAUNTED HOUSE written in an orange, swirly font.

"Look, tell you what," his dad said, getting down on one knee. He put a hand on Jackson's shoulder just like he used to when Jackson got in trouble with his mother and he was the voice of reason whenever she blew up. The comforting hand on his shoulder reminded him of what things were like before the divorce, before the courts ruled he had to live with his mom and could only see his dad every other weekend. "We'll go in together. None of this solo stuff. That was the plan anyway. Did you really think I'd let you go in there alone?"

Jackson cast his gaze to the ground. Sadly, he *did* think his dad wanted him to go in all by himself. He nodded and had to bite back the tears.

"I'd never do that. I was going to go with you. Just needed you to be brave," his dad said. "Okay?"

"I guess."

"That's my boy."

Going into the haunted house was like being asked to go into the girls' bathroom and, come to think of it, the girls' bathroom *was* more appealing than this.

Coming to the carnival had been his dad's idea. Jackson had wanted to go to the toy store because his father got him something every time. Sometimes it was big, sometimes small, but it was always something and there was a certain LEGO City set he had his eye on for a long time.

They'd only been here for maybe an hour, having wandered the grounds, done a few rides. The bumper cars were all right.

No clowns though, which suited Jackson just fine. After catching *The Dark Knight* on TV a few weekends ago and watching the Joker terrorize Gotham, he could do just fine without any maniacal clowns, thank you very much. He didn't care what their intention or purpose. Just. No. Clowns.

His father stood, gripped his boy's hand, and tugged him toward the entrance where the teen with pale skin manning the door waited with arms crossed as if he didn't want to be there any more than Jackson did.

Jackson's heart picked up speed every step of the way, and when he glanced up and saw that green-skinned goblin with yellow eyes looming over the haunted house sign, his heartbeat jumped into a gallop.

A set of four stone steps led into the place. There was no door. Just a black void, nothing but shadow.

Jackson looked around, hoping maybe others were in line behind them and he could be polite and let them go ahead, buy himself some time.

They were the only ones in line.

He couldn't blame anyone for not wanting to come in here.

Oddly, he couldn't hear any sounds coming from within. He'd only been past another haunted house a couple years ago and that one had screams and booms and creepy scratching noises leaking from the doorway.

Not this one. This one was silent.

Jackson couldn't help but wonder if there was a reason.

At the foot of the steps, Jackson's dad showed the teen the carnival wristbands they each wore, and when the teen nodded, his father led him up the steps.

One.

Two.

Three.

Jackson paused. When his foot touched the fourth step, that would be it. He'd be six inches from the shadowy entrance and, because of his dad being a step ahead of him, his dad would already be in.

There'd be no turning back.

Jackson inadvertently tugged on his father's arm.

When his dad turned, he looked annoyed. "What is it?"

He had hoped his father would see the fear on his face, but his old man simply glanced to the sky as if rolling his eyes. "Come on. It'll be okay. You can stay right beside me. Be strong. Don't be afraid."

"I don't want to be, but don't know how *not* to be."

His father's features warmed. "It's simple. You simply choose not to be afraid, and even if your heart jumps or you start to shake, you press on anyway. Being brave is going forward even if you're scared. You think Batman doesn't get scared sometimes?"

"He never gets scared."

"Oh, believe me. I know about that stuff. He gets scared. Some argue he does what he does because he's afraid."

"Of bad guys? That doesn't make sense."

"Of what the bad guys do to people. He faces them anyway, knowing the bad things they do is far worse than any fear they try to portray."

"I don't know what 'portray' means."

"It means to show something. You need to be brave like Batman. You learn to be strong now, you'll grow up strong and you can help others be strong, too." He sighed. "Trust me."

Jackson didn't completely understand all that he meant, but it kind of made sense. Be strong. Go forward. Be like Batman.

Done.

Jackson slowly raised his foot to the fourth step. Once it was planted, he brought up the other one.

Hanging on to his father's hand, the two entered the shadow.

2

At first, there was nothing but darkness, but judging by the way his father led him via a gentle pull on the hand, Jackson was being taken through a series of short, L-shaped hallways before a faint purple light lit an upcoming room. Even after being in the dark for so short a time, Jackson had to squint when he entered the room with the purple light, only to be greeted by a short mannequin of a gray-skinned ghoul with blood around its mouth and wearing a tattered tuxedo.

"Welcome, welcome," it said, its voice scratchy and high. "This is the house, this is the place, the house that will make you scream off your face!" The thing shrieked and Jackson's heart skipped a beat.

"Ah, it's only pretend," his dad said, leaning in close to his ear.

The two walked past the mannequin and Jackson swore the thing looked at him while he did.

They entered the room proper and the purple light faded a little. On either side were glass shelves with dead heads upon them behind a sheet of glass like a giant aquarium. Skeletal fish swam around the heads, some stopping to pick at the flesh, while others swam in circles in one spot. The eyes of some of the deceased were rolled up in their sockets. Some had their eyes closed. Some had their mouths open, jaws slack. Some were missing their jaws entirely.

Just be brave, just be brave, Jackson told himself, and his gaze lingered on the head of a man with no hair, one eye closed, the other open, the iris drooped to the side.

A skeletal fish darted toward the glass then backed away.

Maybe it's afraid of me? Jackson thought. "Are those fish real?"

"Hm?" His father had seemed mesmerized by the faces. He bent down. "What?"

Jackson pointed to the glass. "Are those fish real?"

"Nah. They're robots or something. If it's a skeleton, it's dead. Anyway, come on."

As Jackson left the room with the heads, he thought he saw a white face pop up behind the head of the bald, dead man.

* * *

Walking slowly, Jackson and his dad entered the next room, this one lit up blood red. On either side were strips of yellow police do-not-cross tape, spanning the length of the room. On the left were stacks of dog corpses, their guts ripped open and spilled on the floor, dried blood around their entrails. Animatronic cats bobbed their heads up and down over the bodies, as if eating them and enjoying their victory over their arch-nemeses. Across the floor holographic mice and cockroaches scurried back and forth.

On the right was an empty baby carriage. The wails of an unattended child rang out. Taking a deep breath and summoning his courage, Jackson let go of his father's hand to go and see. When he peered over the strip of tape and over the edge of the carriage, a jolt shot through his chest when he saw a baby doll laying there, one eye hanging out of its socket, a crow inside the carriage beside it, picking at the eye with its beak.

A mannequin of a crying mother sat cross-legged on the ground beside the carriage, slightly rocking back and forth, face in her hands. The echo of her recorded wails made Jackson's heart ache. He supposed not seeing her face was a good thing because, if her auburn scraggily hair was any indicator, she'd probably be spooky to look at.

Some ten feet away from the mother was a semi-circle of people, all in old-fashioned suits and dresses, gathered around a body on the ground.

Jackson noted his father had just looked at it before moving over to the dead dogs again, so he figured it was safe. He went over and peeked in between the people at the body. The figure wore an orange, baggy jumpsuit. A prisoner? He knew prisoners wore orange jumpsuits from TV. But why did the prisoner have on big red shoes? He looked up the length of the body. The face was white . . . like the one from the room. From the way it was positioned, he could make out the blue curly hair, the red lips.

His eyes went wide.

A clown.

"Nonononono . . ." A quick flash of the Joker went through his mind's eye and he ran and grabbed his father's arm.

"Whoa, are you okay?" his dad asked.

"Yeah, fine," he said even though he shook his head.

"Yes, no, maybe so?"

He gripped his dad's arm tighter. "I don't know."

His father put his arm around him. "Let's move on. I'm proud of you for being brave."

Jackson wanted to say thanks, but the word caught in his throat.

As he left the room, it felt like the dead clown was watching him.

3

Shaking off the shivers from the previous room, but not letting go of his dad's hand, Jackson braced himself for the next place. This one was lit in gray, and he suddenly felt like he'd just been transported into a black-and-white movie. He glanced up at his father; his dad's skin was awash with gray. He checked his dad's hands. They were gray, too. He searched the ceiling for the lights but didn't see any. On either side of a woodchip-laden path was a fake forest with birch trees and dead pines; no leaves were on the birch, and pine needles skirted the base of the others.

A loud screech pierced Jackson's ears when a stuffed raccoon moved on a sliding track behind the trees from one side of the room to the other. A bear roared on a speaker somewhere. Upon closer inspection, the birch trees had chipmunks with dead, white eyes eating big hairy spiders. A few bats flapped their wings as they swirled about the top of the room. Jackson didn't know if they were on strings or . . . no, they couldn't be real . . . but the way the moved in circles and dipped up and down—maybe.

Hanging from the pines on the other side of the room were baby heads, strung up like Christmas tree ornaments. All of them had big, wide-open eyes and blood leaking out the corners of their mouths. Presents were gathered under one of the pines, covered in tattered paper. One of them had a big bow, just like the one Jackson had gotten for Christmas from his grandma last year. Eyes fixed on the package, his ears faintly picked up the click-click-clicking of mechanical gears and then . . . BAM! The present with the bow popped open and a goblin's head burst out, mouth agape, tongue hanging out. Jackson yelled and backed up a few steps. The goblin's head bobbed up and down on the coiled wire. It was the same goblin that was on the sign outside.

"Dad!" he shouted. He turned around but he was in the gray forest room alone. Heart immediately jumping into high speed, Jackson spun around a full three-sixty on his heels. "Dad!"

Something was looking at him.

Jackson turned.

It was the goblin, still bouncing on the coiled wire.

From behind, the shuffling of feet. Relief washed over him.

"Dad!" he said and turned around. Except his dad wasn't there, just the trees on the other side of the room . . . and the humanoid shadow beyond them. "You shouldn't be back there," he told his father.

When the figure came around from the other

side of the tree, a lump formed in Jackson's throat at the drooping white face, the big dark gray lips and curly gray hair.

It wore a jumpsuit, which he guessed without the lighting was probably orange.

Screaming, Jackson ran straight ahead into the dark archway that led into the next room.

* * *

No lights. Just dark. Jackson stopped and turned around, hoping to see the gray light coming from the previous room. He couldn't see anything, not even the hand in front of his face.

"Dad!" His heart slammed against his ribcage and his legs turned to rubber. "Dad! Help me! Where are you?"

No answer, not a sound.

He stood there, tears gushing from his eyes, screaming for his father, only to be greeted by silence in return. After he screamed himself hoarse, he coughed and thought he was going to throw up. Wiping the tears from his eyes, he simply stood there, shaking.

Why would his dad leave him?

Did something happen to him?

Was this his plan all along? To take him into this place only to take off? Was that why his father insisted he go in here?

Jackson closed his eyes and forced himself to breathe slowly. *What would Batman do?* He thought about it. *He'd try to find a way out. He'd use his night vision and find the door. Except I don't have any night vision and I don't know where the door is.*

A touch on his shoulder startled him and made him yelp and jump away. "Who's there? Dad?" He wanted to cry again but fought against the tears in an effort to be brave.

A moment later, the hand was on his shoulder again, just like his dad had done to him outside. Was his father kneeling in front of him? Could he reach out, lean forward and fall into his father's arms?

Jackson felt along the hand, up the sleeve, and realized his dad was standing. He rushed into him and grabbed hold of his legs in a bear hug. The sharp scent of paint pierced his nose and he wondered if his dad had stepped in something.

Whatever the next room was, he didn't care. He just wanted his dad to take him back through the house and out of here.

"I want to go home. Take me home. I don't want to see this stuff anymore," Jackson said.

The hand left his shoulder and gently pulled him off the legs. It took him by the arm. They walked forward in the dark.

Jackson said, "I don't want to go into the next room. Let's go back. Take me home."

They kept walking forward. Maybe they *were* going back? He probably got himself turned around in the dark. Besides, his dad knew how scared he was and how much he hadn't wanted to go into the haunted house in the first place. His father was probably taking him back the way they came in. Any second now they'd be back in the gray room, in that forest.

Why wasn't his dad saying anything, though?

As they stepped further through the dark, the accordion sound of carnival music began to fill Jackson's ears. They were going outside! Was the all-black room the end of the haunted house? Really? Finally?

"Awesome!" he said.

The music grew louder.

The sound of a door opening rose up in front of him. When it opened completely, orange and yellow light greeted him. He squinted against it and looked at the hand holding his arm.

It was white.

4

The room was a tent, big and orange with yellow stripes running from the sides and meeting at the center at the top. Scattered across the pebbled ground were a series of black cages with iron bars, at least fifty of them, each containing a child, most Jackson's age.

Jackson couldn't move from fear, his feet planted, legs like tree trunks.

The clown stood beside him but Jackson kept his eyes to the ground, unable to bring himself to look the figure in the eye.

"Welcome to the carnival," it whispered.

How he hadn't seen the giant big top behind the haunted house, Jackson didn't know. Those trees in front, they must've hidden it from view.

Two white fingers filled Jackson's vision, paused just in front of his eyes, before making their way down under his chin. Firmly, they guided his face up and to the left until his gaze settled upon the clown. Even through the blur of tears, Jackson made out the chalk-white face, the big red lips that had looked black in the forest room, the clown's eyes void of white. They were black almonds sitting in deeply recessed sockets. The blue hair, which had looked gray in the other room, sat in a ragged mess atop the clown's head.

"Wh-where's my d-dad?" Jackson asked.

The clown looked at him and simply shook his head.

What did that mean? That he was gone? Dead? No, not dead! "Dad!"

He felt all eyes in the room look at him. He glanced over at the children in the cages. They were of all ages, some his own, others younger. One looked to be about the same age as the teen working the door outside. Upon further inspection, Jackson realized all the children in the cages had white faces.

Clowns in red, blue, green and yellow jumpsuits milled about, walking around the cages, some kicking the bars with their big floppy shoes. A couple others had clubs and banged on the cages, forcing the children within to back up to the other side, only to be startled when another clown came up and hit the bars behind them.

One clown walking past said, "Welcome, welcome, this is the house, this is the place, the house that will make you scream off your face."

It was the same jingle the ghoul mannequin said when Jackson and his father first entered the haunted house.

Jackson's legs gave out from under him, tears dripping from his face and running onto his knees.

5

It was impossible to sleep in the cage, the iron bars against the pebbled floor making a terrible bed. There was nothing else in them. Jackson didn't know how long he'd been in here. His stomach growled; he was hungry, thirsty, and he wondered if he'd ever get out of here. The thought he was dreaming had already crossed his mind, but despite all efforts to wake up, even so far as smacking his head against the cage bars, nothing worked.

The clown that brought him was across the room, looking in on one of the children, a young girl with blonde hair. She looked tired and he wondered if she'd ever slept since she got here, whenever that was.

"Psst . . ." A whisper from behind him.

Jackson didn't want to turn around in case it was one of the clowns.

"Psst . . . hey!"

Jackson shook his head.

"Over here!" The whisper was higher in tone, clearly belonging to a kid.

Jackson turned.

The boy in the cage beside him had dark hair that hung just above his blue eyes, his skin white, his lips blue, maybe from being cold.

"It's okay, don't cry," the boy said.

"I'm not crying," Jackson said and wiped his eyes.

"What's your name?"

Jackson wasn't sure if he should give his name. His mom taught him long ago never to give his name to strangers and, sometimes, she said, even to other kids. This seemed like one of those times. "I'm not telling."

"That's okay. I'm Bonzo," the boy said.

"Bonzo?"

"Yeah. That's what they call me."

"Who?"

"The clowns."

"What's your real name?"

"I—" The boy furrowed his brow. "I'm . . . I'm . . ." He shook his head. "I'm Bonzo. That's my name."

"That can't be your name."

"Well, it is."

That's a stupid name. That's a . . . that's a clown's name. What was this place?

The loud clang of metal on metal jolted Jackson out of his conversation. The clown that brought him here stood in front of his cage and glared at him. With a finger to his nose, the clown said, "Shhh . . ." then moved on.

When the clown was a good distance away, Bonzo whispered, "They don't want us talking."

"Why not?" Jackson whispered back.

"They said it's more fun for the audience if we stay quiet."

"What?"

"They said the people who watch us will like us more if we don't say anything and just act. You do know how to act, don't you?"

There was something seriously wrong with this kid. Why did he seem so excited to be here?

"I don't act," Jackson said. "Where you're daddy?"

"Over there," Bonzo said and nodded toward the clown that brought Jackson in.

"That's your dad?"

"He's everyone's dad and the other ones are my brothers. When we're old enough, we can come out of our boxes and perform for people."

Boxes? Did he mean the cages? Was this place where someone went to become a clown?

"Do you know where my dad is?" Jackson asked.

"Yeah."

"Really?"

"For sure. Always."

"Always?"

"Your dad is my dad. You're my new brother."

Jackson shook his head and shouted, "No, you're not, and that clown isn't my dad!"

Heavy footfalls on the pebbly ground rushed toward his cage as the clown in the orange jumpsuit marched toward him.

"Father Clown!" Bonzo shouted.

"Shhh . . ." Father Clown said.

"Sorry," Bonzo whispered.

Father Clown nodded then unlocked Jackson's cage and hauled him out.

Bonzo joyfully waved at him as he was pulled away.

Jackson pulled against the clown's strong grip, only to encounter resistance every step of the way as he was dragged from the room.

6

Father Clown's smooth white fingers touched Jackson's forehead, his cheeks, his chin. It was only when the clown's hands were this close did Jackson notice how smooth and glossy they were, how big.

He sat in a chair in a dark room, the only light a spotlight shining down on them from above. The clown sat across from him, a bucket of white paint beside him.

"I want my dad," Jackson said.

"Shhh . . ."

"Stop shushing me!"

The clown didn't reply, but instead raised a finger as if asking for him to wait a moment, then popped open the can of white paint beside his chair. Its sharp scent filled the air around them and caused Jackson's head to spin and eyes to droop. His heartrate picked up, beat real fast, then slowed as calm overtook him, the smell pointed but intoxicating.

He could fall asleep in this chair.

He started to pitch forward, but the clown gently pushed him back upright and, with one hand on his shoulder, helped him maintain the position.

The clown dipped the fingers of his free hand in the paint then gently applied it to

Jackson's face. The paint's smell grew stronger and his head swam even more.

He had been thinking about somebody. Someone important. He could no longer remember who.

It started with a D. That was all he knew.

The cool paint sent a shiver across his skin each time the clown touched him, but as more was applied, the calmer he became. When the clown was done, his face felt cold, and already his skin began to tighten as the paint started to dry. It was like wearing a mask and he felt protected by it.

The clown sat back in the chair and looked Jackson over, studied him, then said, "Mervo."

* * *

The mornings were all the same: be let out of the cage, led away to the side room to have his face painted, then, after, a day of practice. Clown cars, juggling, tumbling, running, honking noses and winking.

They were all preparation, Father Clown said. Preparation for something great, something special.

Special performances, ones requiring soft hands and gentle movements yet all with an edge that asserted authority.

Mornings.

Paintings.

The intoxicating and soothing smell of the white paint coating Mervo's skin.

Breathe in.

Breathe out.

His head grew lighter by the day, thoughts and memories quickly vanishing and escaping until, when he tried looking back on his life, all he saw in his mind's eye was a white fog.

Father Clown said all great clowns came from the white fog. It was what made them unique, what separated them from the run-of-the-mill clowns of other carnivals.

Time slipped away, oozed, was painted.

Mervo's face grew heavier with each layer of paint applied, but his heart, his mind—those were free.

Free to be whatever Father Clown wanted him to be.

* * *

Four years later . . .

Father Clown led Mervo through a hallway lined with circus posters, each one highlighting one of the senior clowns, all depicted in the midst of one clown feat or another: juggling, escaping a clown car, honking horns, or having a cigar explode when trying to light it.

At the end of the hallway was another door, a wooden one, with a tarnished brass doorknob, seemingly worn from years of use.

Father Clown paused before opening the door and made the hand sign for "First."

This was Mervo's first performance. He wasn't nervous—the soothing scent of the paint took care of that—but he wanted to do Father Clown proud.

He opened the door. They went in.

The room was dark and reminded Mervo of the same room he got his paint on every morning. In the middle of the room was a chair with a man tied to it, hands bound behind his back.

Father Clown rounded to the front of the man, eyed the fellow in the chair, then signaled for Mervo to come join him. Mervo did and when he looked at the man in the chair, the fellow seemed familiar but he couldn't quite place him. Blue eyes, a black baseball hat with a picture of a brown cartoon dog on it.

The man's eyes were wide with fear, his voice muffled behind the duct tape.

With a jab of his index finger toward the ground, Father Clown signaled for Mervo to stay there. After, Father Clown rounded to the back of the man. Gently, he laid his hand across the man's forehead. For a moment Mervo wondered if the white paint on Father Clown's smooth hands would smear, but it didn't. Father Clown pulled back on the man's head, pulled out a knife from behind his back, and handed it to Mervo.

Mervo took it, then watched as Father Clown drew his finger across the man's neck.

Slice. That was the instruction.

Mervo nodded and brought the knife across the man's neck, drawing a line of red across his trachea. When he finished the maneuver, he brought his hand up in a quick, jerking motion, palm upward, just like he did when juggling. Blood gushed out and ran across the blade and down the man's chest. The fellow's body jerked and his head flopped further back. Father Clown drew his finger across the neck again, the tip of his finger grazing the new opening. Mervo brought the blade across again, cutting further through the muscles and tendons that once held the head in place. Again he jerked the knife, this time palm down, as if slapping his knee, nyuk, nyuk. More blood leaked out as he did so. Once done, Father Clown drew his finger across the neck one more time. Mervo obeyed, and finished cutting through the neck, severing the head completely. Father Clown let it drop into his hands and he cradled it in his arms like a newborn baby. With a nod, he let Mervo know he did a good job and held out his hand for the knife. Mervo gave it to him.

The man's head faced Mervo and the gaze on his face seemed one of . . . disappointment.

* * *

Dance, my child
Dance for me
Embrace the darkness
Your destiny

This one screamed against the gag while Mervo brandished the knife. Her brown eyes were wide, the whites dwarfing the irises they were open so big. When he came in and brought the blade across her throat, her whole body locked. Warm blood gushed out onto his hand, turning the skin a deep crimson. Father Clown held the woman's head tight as he instructed to bring the blade across again. The woman's neck was so small that all it took was a quick, second swipe and her head came off completely.

The lights dimmed.

The show was over.

* * *

Dance, my child
Dance for me
Embrace your courage
Your ecstasy

The old man sat there, chest puffed, chin jutting out, as if defying Mervo to make a move. The man wasn't putting up a fight, but Mervo could see the guy's legs quivering as he sat bound to the chair.

Those looking on from the two-way mirror were no doubt excited about what was to come. Mervo was, too, and he was more than eager to please Father Clown by removing this old guy's head.

He'd do it slowly.

The first pass of the blade was just enough to break the skin and cause mild bleeding, but not enough to do any more damage. It no doubt stung, and Mervo knew it did because the man's huffing intensified against the duct tape.

Mervo drew the blade back, and cut through a second time, this one going a little harder, a little deeper. More blood oozed out, but he'd grown skilled enough with the blade to not as yet sever a major artery. Each time he juggled, prepping for each performance, only increased his hand-eye coordination and swiftness of hand.

Again he brought the knife across, this time nicking the aorta. Blood spurted out in a wild arc, creating a line of red against his yellow-and-green flower-patterned overalls. The man started to shake in his seat.

Bringing the blade across for the fourth time, Mervo was careful to only do it ever so slightly. The man was clearly in pain, and was losing blood fast.

Things weren't going as planned.

It was supposed to be slow.

Mervo tried again, this time just grazing the knife across the opening. He glanced up at

Father Clown; his eyes were fixed on the damage being done to the man's throat while he held the man's head.

One more time, and the blade broke through the aorta and blood sprayed everywhere.

Frustrated, Mervo brought the knife across the throat hard and quick and took the head off in one violent swing. Father Clown stumbled back with the head in his arms, blood squirting from the base of the head; crimson liquid shot upward like a water fountain from the neck of the corpse in the chair.

Mervo knew he'd be confined to his cage for at least two weeks for screwing up.

More was expected of him now.

* * *

Dance, my child
Dance for me
Embrace your heritage
Your legacy

Seventeen strokes with the blade.

A slow kill.

The blood gently leaked out the sides of her neck, cascaded over her shoulders like a shawl.

The girl's head gently fell into Father Clown's arms.

Mervo was getting good at this.

The Dance of Mervo and Father Clown

* * *

Dance, my child
Dance for me
Embrace who I am
Your father, you'll see

She seemed to be the business type, hair up in a bun, glasses, fine suit with matching skirt. Mervo knew, from Father Clown's disclosures, these were the same kind of people who paid to watch the performances.

Trembling in her chair, hands bound behind her, duct tape over her mouth like the others, the woman's wide eyes said she clearly knew what was coming. Oh, maybe not specifically, but she knew it'd be bad.

It'd been a year since Mervo's seventeen-stroke kill. Now he was up to twenty-six. If he could hit thirty with this woman, Mervo would be pleased and Father Clown would no doubt be pleased as well. He'd practiced his juggling, not just with balls but with batons as well. He was more flexible, too, from all the somersaults, the stretching, the odd positions in the clown car.

The woman eyed the blade the whole time, tears running out of the corners of her eyes, smearing her mascara, the makeup creating stars around her eyes like a harlequin.

Mervo brought the blade across. The woman choked, but not from blood. It was barely a scratch but enough to startle her. He drew the knife across again, this time from the other side. A little bit of blood leaked out.

The woman shrieked against the duct tape and bent her head forward, as if trying to hide the target. Father Clown jerked her head back.

Mervo hated it when they screamed and didn't cooperate.

He brought the blade across, deepening the incision.

Strokes three and four drew more blood. By stroke seven, she finally stopped screaming, as if realizing the constant pulsing of her neck muscles from her cries only made it worse.

Once Mervo hit strokes fifteen, sixteen and seventeen, he was about a third of the way through. Blood flowed evenly out of the opening like a fondue fountain, running down the front and sides of the woman like a blanket. She was still alive, but not for long. He had managed to avoid the major arteries for the most part, but had cut her windpipe. Soon she'd die from oxygen deprivation and drown in her own blood.

Stroke nineteen went especially smooth, as did twenty and twenty-one.

Only five more to tie, he thought. Once at twenty-four, he braced himself as he was almost through.

He was so excited and a part of him wanted to cleave the head right off and let Father Clown catch it and make his nod of approval . . . but to make it to thirty—he could only imagine how proud Father Clown would be if he could pull it off.

He brought the knife across, barely cutting, but drew more blood.

He did it again. Twenty-six. Tied.

Once more and stroke twenty-seven produced a fresh flow of blood. The woman's heart must be racing. Her eyes were closed, but she wasn't dead, not with the blood still bubbling up and over like it was.

Strokes twenty-eight and twenty-nine were oh so delicate.

Stroke thirty.

He expected the head to roll off into Father Clown's arms, but it still hung out by a thin layer of skin and flesh.

Mervo brought the knife across and finished the job.

Thirty-one.

A new record.

7

Mervo sat in his cage, legs drawn up, wrists resting on his knees. He looked over at Bonzo, who sat the same way. They didn't talk anymore, not since Father Clown outlawed speaking altogether. It didn't matter, though. Clowns weren't supposed to talk. What mattered was action.

Father Clown came over and banged on his cage. Three bangs. Mervo knew what that meant: it was time to get painted. The white paint was applied, layer after layer, every day. It had grown so thick on his face that sometimes its weight would cause his face to droop forward and the skin to pull on his flesh.

As he followed Father Clown past the cages to the room beyond, Mervo was pleased that even more brothers and sisters had joined them since he first got here.

He sat down on the chair across from Father Clown like always, and waited for a fresh layer of paint to be applied. The paint's smell was so good and so comforting. All his cares and worry about the performance to come disappeared with each application and made following Father Clown's instruction so much easier.

As Father Clown applied the paint, Mervo raised his hands, made one stiff like a board, the other in a C-shape, and brought them together, the first below the latter. A clown's question mark. He then parted his hands and drew them out to either side, palms up.

What are we going to do today? was the question.

Father Clown taught him the signs, so he understood. When he finished applying the paint, he squeezed his fists together a few inches apart and rocked them side-to-side.

Driving. Clown car.

Everyone would pile in and there they'd remain until he came and got them. Sometimes it would only last a few minutes. Other times over a day. The lesson was to live in the moment, stay focused, ignore discomfort.

Mervo nodded.

Father Clown brought his fingers to his own face, touched his cheeks, then pulled the hands away, palms out.

All done.

Mervo tried to smile, but the layers of paint made moving his cheeks impossible.

Once back in his cage, he watched as Father Clown took Bonzo to get his face done.

Good for Bonzo. The layers of paint on Bonzo's face had caused his cheeks to droop below his chin line, his lips pulled down at the corners in a permanent frown. The skin under his eyes was also pulled down, causing the flesh underneath the whites of his eyes to be red and inflamed.

It was beautiful.

He couldn't wait to be crammed up against his friend in the clown car.

8

One by one Mervo and his brothers and sisters went into the clown car. Its seats were removed, so was most of the interior; it was lined with nails and screws, each pointing inward. These were for discipline, Father Clown had said, to learn comfort once back in the cages.

Mervo was on his side, in the trunk, his body conformed to the curves of the trunk's interior. He was to always face the inside of the car, and he always had. Same with the others. Everyone faced each other or faced into each other. This built unity amongst the family.

Bonzo came up beside him and nestled in, his backside pressed up against Mervo's thighs. Since Bonzo was flexible, his legs went against the side of the car, lining up with the walls in the small space.

As the others came in and positioned themselves, Mervo caught a new face joining them, one he hadn't seen before. It was little boy, his skin seeming to have received its first coat of paint earlier that morning.

The boy was brought in close to him, his feet by Mervo's head. Whimpering, the boy got into position, clearly unsure of himself and what to do. Since they couldn't talk, Mervo reached out, and when his white-painted hands touched the boy's leg, the boy jerked his feet back.

Mervo waved then, with each index finger, gesticulated a smile across his cheeks. He then did the same for the boy. The boy smiled and it was the first time Mervo had seen a smile in a long, long time. As gently as he could, he showed the boy what to do and where to put his legs. Across the way, just on the other side of the door, Father Clown looked on in approval and Mervo was happy he was doing such a good job.

As the clowns finished getting in, it grew darker inside the vehicle until, finally, all light was blocked and twenty of them were alone in the car. With a big thud, the door slammed closed.

As they all lay there, squished in silence, Mervo's ears perked up to the sound of the boy's whimpering. He tapped the boy's feet in an effort to give him comfort, but the boy jerked and kicked hard against Mervo's face, forcing part of it to twist and press against the nails lining the inside of the vehicle.

Neck bent at an odd angle and pressure mounting at the base of his skull, Mervo tried to get back to his original position. When he moved his cheek, it was stuck, the nails having embedded themselves in the layers of paint on his face. Unable to move, he gave in and just stayed there, waiting.

Time passed.

The boy began to cry. Someone shushed him.

Mervo tried to reach and tap the boy's leg, again to reassure him it would be all right, that this exercise was for his own good and would make him a better clown. The boy jerked his leg again, squishing Mervo's face up against the nails even more.

Something pulled on his skin as his head turned even further to the left, causing a deep pain in the side of his neck. He had to fix himself or he wouldn't last, even after all his practice doing this. Father Clown taught him the right way to be in a car, not like this with his face and neck twisted.

Mervo slowly began to turn his head to straighten it, the layers of paint on his skin catching and pulling against the nails. With each turn, the paint scraped against the nails, yanked against his skin. It burned deep and a gush of liquid flushed over his skin somewhere in between it and the paint. Blood?

Oh no. My face! he thought. *It must be white. It has to stay white! No!*

Panicking, he pulled and tugged against the nails and started thrashing around in the little space he had until, with a violent rip, the paint peeled away and a wet warmth covered his skin.

For the first time in years, Mervo started to cry, his tears mixing with the blood.

9

Back in his cage, Mervo hid his face from the others. They couldn't see him like this. Not without the paint. Without it . . . he was nobody, for what was a clown unless he had a white face?

The stinging remained and came in waves of heat across what was left of his skin. The exposed flesh was tender to the air and every time he touched it or it brushed up against something, it burned like all get out. Father Clown had used a few old rags to wipe the wounds, but the look on the clown's face said Mervo's time as a clown was over.

It was night and the other clowns slept. Bonzo lay curled up on his side, snoring away like he always did. It was the only time he was allowed to "speak." The boy from earlier whimpered as he slept, each little squeak resonating deep within Mervo.

It sounded familiar.

It reminded him of something.

Of someone.

He missed the smell of the paint and the way it made him feel. It peeled away all fear and worry, and his mind was always clear. Now his head hurt, and not from the pain on his face. Thoughts began leaking in, ones to do with a gray forest, some sort of purple light, something about a tuxedo.

Mervo leaned his head back against the cage bars and closed his eyes.

* * *

A man was with him as Mervo walked through the dark. His smell, the scent of—he couldn't remember—but it was familiar, comforting.

A hand on his shoulder, a touch he hadn't felt in a long, long time.

As they wandered through the dark, Mervo said, "I don't want to go in there."

"So, what, you're going to spend the rest of your life afraid?"

That voice. It didn't belong to Father Clown.

* * *

Mervo woke up with a start, sweat beading his brow. Some must've dripped down along his cheeks because they stung like crazy. That voice in his dream. He *knew* that voice. Who was it? It couldn't have been his imagination. Every dream he could recall was always about Father Clown or what they did to prepare for each show.

It was still night and everyone else was asleep. He glanced over in Bonzo's direction and half-expected to see a child with bangs hanging as low as his eyes. Instead, he saw the laying figure of someone around his same size, snoring away.

"Bonzo . . ." he whispered. *Did I just speak?* His voice sounded different than how he thought it should. He gently cleared his throat and tried again. "Bonzo." His voice cracked and he swallowed a dry lump. "He told me his name was Bonzo."

* * *

Come morning, one of Father Clown's assistants came by, a black bag of leftover popcorn hanging by a strap from his neck. When he approached Mervo's cage, he tossed some in—four handfuls—eyed Mervo as if sizing up his injury, then moved on. Another clown would be by with water shortly.

Last night's sleep—well, there hadn't been much, not with each dream seemingly more than just make believe. One was Halloween, walking down someone's driveway, a bag of candy in one hand with a grownup's in the other, except when Mervo looked up at the grownup, the person didn't have a face. He *did* know them, though.

He slowly chewed the popcorn, the day-old butter coating his tongue and the inside of his cheeks. He'd grown used to having to be patient for the water.

Bonzo was in his own cage and Mervo wondered if today would be a day of practice or a day of performing.

Are those fish real? The thought came out of nowhere. The reply: *Nah. They're robots or something. If it's a skeleton, it's dead.* That voice again. Head full and achy, Mervo tried to think where he'd heard that voice before.

What's your name? It sounded a lot like Bonzo.

"I won't tell you my name," Mervo said. *My mother told me never to tell strangers my name.*

Then it hit him.

He had a mother.

A mother clown or just . . . someone else?

* * *

Father Clown surveyed Mervo's face as he sat in the chair, the can of white paint at his feet. The man seemed concerned though his expression never showed it. The layers of paint concealed everything.

Father Clown slowly shook his head.

Mervo raised his eyebrows for the first time in over a year. Father Clown must've noticed because he cocked his head to the side.

Mervo so desperately wanted to speak, but if he did, he didn't know how Father Clown would react, so instead he gestured with his hands, palms up, then brought them to his face and moved them in a circle around his cheeks, his forehead. *More paint?*

The clown sat back in his chair, crossed his

arms, and shook his head.

Mervo made the driving signal.

Father Clown shook his head.

He held out his hands palms up and alternated them up and down, juggling invisible balls.

Father Clown shook his head again.

Then it *was* over.

Mervo thought he'd be devastated, but instead felt relieved.

A rush of dizziness swept over him and he tumbled out of his chair.

* * *

Back in his cage, Mervo waited for Bonzo to return from performing.

Waited.

Bonzo seemed to have been gone a long time.

Waited.

He'd been gone a long time.

Waiting.

Poor Bonzo had been gone for a long . . .

Waiting . . .

The white paint, though only absent for about a day, felt like it'd been gone for a long time.

Waiting.

Bonzo . . . Mervo . . . had been gone a long time.

He'd been waiting.

Jackson had been waiting for a long time.
Jackson.
Waiting.
Long time.

10

My name is Jackson. "My name is Jackson!"

Mervo—Jackson—snapped his hand to his mouth.

"Dad!" he said into his fingers.

His dad was gone. His dad left him.

Left him!

In the dark.

Jackson looked to the entrance of the big top. It was there he'd come through with Father Clown several years ago. Why hadn't he remembered that? What changed?

He thought back to his conversation with Bonzo when he first arrived and how it seemed Bonzo was reading a script.

Something *had* happened to him. To both of them.

Something to do with his place, the clowns, the white paint.

Then it was clear. The paint. It was what controlled him. Something about it made him susceptible to whatever he was told; changed his feelings, his thoughts, who he was.

His memory as a clown remained. He remembered the people. Remembered their screams.

Remembered each performance.

Why? How could any of this happen? Who

was letting the clowns do this? Did Father Clown have control over everyone? Come to think of it, everyone who worked at the carnival had white faces. He didn't think anything of it, as some had it on so faintly it looked like they simply had pale skin. Others, it was more apparent and he thought they'd been wearing makeup. But here, with the clowns, the layers of paint . . .

Father Clown was making his rounds again, moving about the cages, supervising the children. The other clowns milled about, each one in a trance.

Finally, Bonzo was escorted back to his cage. He was let in and sat down. The clown that brought him back closed the cage door.

I have to get out of here, Jackson thought. *I need my dad. Where is he?*

* * *

The skin on Jackson's face stretched and pulled every time he moved his facial muscles. Each wince only reminded him of what he'd been doing for the past four years and the pain he inflicted on others.

His dad. Had he killed him when he was under Father Clown's control? Was there a way to know?

The schedule under the Big Top was very strict, and only when Father Clown let him out of his cage to go practice with the others would he have a chance to escape.

So Jackson waited, heart aching, wondering after the fate of his father.

Bonzo was awake and sat there, back against the cage, white face staring straight ahead, lost in the haze the paint invoked. Jackson wondered if he could take Bonzo with him. He wouldn't go willingly, however, not with his face still painted. And to remove it, after all these years of buildup, it'd probably tear the flesh right off just like it had him.

The senior clowns milled about the cages, shuffling their feet. Eventually, Father Clown appeared and began opening the doors. From the movement of his hands, Jackson saw today they'd be platform jumping, bouncing off teeter-totters, and doing somersaults again.

All conditioning. Preparation. Coordination. Transferable skills to torture and murder.

Murder.

Tears leaked from the corners of his eyes.

The things he'd done . . .

If only the people who came to the clown show knew what these little clowns really did and how the real money was made.

Jackson didn't understand all of it, but it seemed the carnival was all a front, owned by some very powerful people who needed other people killed. Those needing to be disposed of would go for a "pleasant afternoon out," be kidnapped, the clowns doing the dirty work while those in charge watched, getting revenge or just bumping someone off because they stepped on the wrong people's toes. Father Clown was in charge, the warden.

Sometimes, kids would be recruited and made to continue the work. And sometimes their families would be taken and killed, too.

People went missing all the time, whether at a fair or out in the street. Buy off the right cops and no one's the wiser.

Father Clown walked past Jackson's cage, opened up Bonzo's, and let him out. He turned, then walked over to Jackson, slowing his gait as he neared the cage, then picked up his pace and walked past.

No, no, no, no, Jackson thought. *He can't leave me here!* He gripped the iron bars of his cage and shook them.

Father Clown stopped and glanced over his shoulder. Jackson made the sign for "Me, too" and waited. The clown seemed to consider his reply, then shook his head.

Does he know the effects of the paint have worn off? He made the gesture for "please." Father Clown still shook his head and went to join the other clowns, leading them away to practice.

"He's going to leave me here to die," Jackson whispered.

* * *

He had to get out of there.

Later, when Bonzo returned and was led back into his cage, Jackson asked if he could have his cage right up next to his friend's.

The clown shook his head.

Jackson asked with his hands, *Please?*

The clown sighed, looked side-to-side, then came forward. He tried maneuvering Jackson's cage to drag it next to Bonzo's, but thanks to Jackson's weight, was having a hard time of it. With a grunt, the clown unlocked the cage and motioned Jackson to come out. He did and stood by as the clown dragged the cage along the gravel and set it right next to Bonzo's. The clown motioned for him to go back in.

Jackson slowly stepped forward, head aching, heart heavy. He knew he had to go and leave this horrible place, but where would he go afterward?

The clown grabbed him by the arm and pulled him toward the cage. Jackson broke free and gestured his compliance.

The clown had a hand on Jackson's back just as he stooped to crawl back into the cage. Quickly, Jackson reached over and grabbed the clown's arm and tugged him down so hard the clown landed in a heap at the cage's entrance. Not wasting anytime, he kicked the clown's head so it was close to the cage's frame and with a howl Jackson slammed the cage door against it, the metal bars smacking and digging into the clown's head with each blow. Soon, Jackson heard a crack as the metal broke the bone, and it wasn't long before the clown's head started caving in on the side taking the impact, blood gushing from the clown's ears and mouth. The clown's body twitched and jerked for a few moments before lying still.

Panting, Jackson slammed the cage door one more time, then looked about. The other senior clowns in the room had taken notice and started coming toward him.

Feral with wave after wave of adrenaline coursing through him, Jackson clawed at his face and tore at whatever remainder of the paint was there. It ripped and pulled at his skin, and when he pulled his hands away, they were covered in blood. He spat it at the clowns and took off, dodging to the right so they wouldn't grab hold of him.

Jackson ran out of the Big Top and straight into the dark.

This was where he lost his father.

Hearing the clamoring of clown shoes behind him, he ran into the gray forest beyond, stopped, and looked for a place to hide. The trees were too skeletal to provide any coverage, so he ran to the next room, red and terrible.

He sped past everything and hit the room beyond, finding the aquarium with the skeleton fish. All those heads on the wall. He recognized some of them. The people he killed, they were there. There was the business woman, and the prideful old man, and the many others whose lives he stole. His heart jumped when he saw his father's head, sitting there on the glass shelf, in between a female's with sunken cheekbones and another woman's with short hair.

"Dad . . ." he said.

Had he done this? Had Father Clown?

Either way, Father Clown had been the one responsible.

Jackson looked to the door. There were the adjoined L-shaped hallways beyond, if he remembered right, then the door leading outside.

Outside. Free. Finally. After all this time.

How he wanted to run, get out of here, but he couldn't do it. Not with his dad's head sitting there, his sunken eyes asking for justice.

A couple of the senior clowns entered the room, then stepped to the side as Father Clown came in between them, his bucket of white paint in his hand.

"You killed my dad!" Jackson said.

Father Clown glanced at the aquarium, then back at Jackson. He shook his head, then pointed at him.

Jackson's eyes went wide and his heart ached. He had half-expected to hear this, but to actually hear it, to find out he killed his dad without remembering every detail . . . . Charging him, he tackled Father Clown to the floor. The two clowns who came in with him immediately went for him, grabbed him by the arms, and brought him to his feet. Father Clown stood up, still gripping the paint bucket.

"No! No more. I don't want it!"

The clown opened the lid and dumped it over Jackson's head, covering him in white paint. Its smell entered his nose and he felt the familiar rush from long ago, the one where his head went dizzy and he began to calm down.

"I can't. Don't turn me into another—"

Father Clown lifted his smooth fingers and began drawing on Jackson's face. He felt the clown trace his eyebrows, his cheeks, drawing in paint from his hair and bringing it to his face.

Eyes closed, Jackson's world tilted and he felt himself fall back. The other clowns must've caught him because he was on the floor. There was pressure on his eyes as the paint was parted by what felt like thumbs.

When he blinked them open, Father Clown stood above him. "Mervo."

About the Author

A.P. Fuchs is the author of many novels and short stories. His most recent books are *Mech Apocalypse; Axiom-man: Outlaw; Axiom-man: Episode No. 2: Underground Crusade; Getting Down and Digital: How to Self-publish Your Book; Look, Up on the Screen! The Big Book of Superhero Movie Reviews; Canadian Scribbler: Collected Letters of an Underground Writer.*

Also a cartoonist, he is known for his superhero series, *The Axiom-man Saga,* both in novel and comic book format.

Fuchs's main website is **www.canisterx.com**

THE
CANISTER X TRANSMISSION

Get it weekly in your inbox

www.tinyletter.com/apfuchs